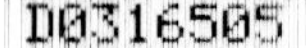

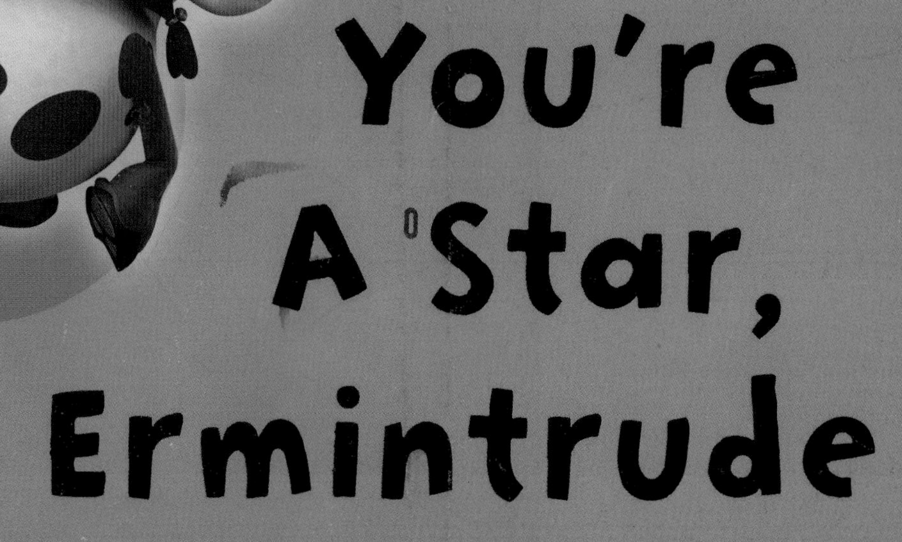

You're A Star, Ermintrude

HarperCollins *Children's Books*

First published in Great Britain in 2005 by HarperCollins Children's Books.
HarperCollins Children's Books is a division of HarperCollins Publishers Ltd.
Creative Consultant Liz Keynes
1 3 5 7 9 10 8 6 4 2

0-00-718357-7
A CIP catalogue for this title is available from the British Library.
The HarperCollins website address is: www.harpercollinschildrensbooks.co.uk
Printed and bound in China

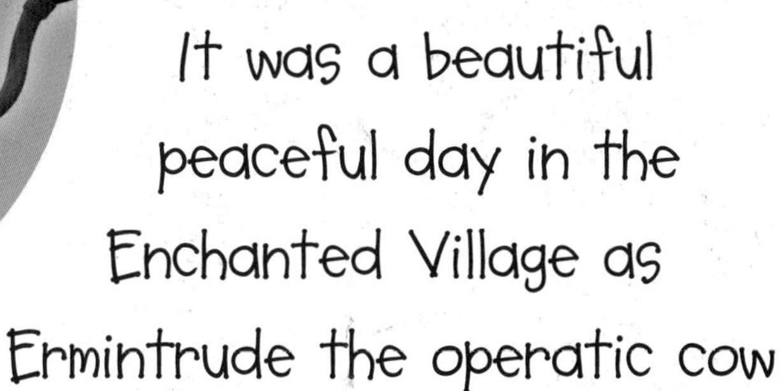

It was a beautiful peaceful day in the Enchanted Village as Ermintrude the operatic cow began practising for her big concert.

"EEOOOO," she bellowed.

The noise was truly terrible! Only Brian the snail thought she sounded wonderful.

Dougal tried to slink past but Ermintrude spotted him.

"Yoohoo!" she trilled loudly. "Coming to my concert?"

"Concert?" said Dougal innocently, backing away as quickly as he could. "What concert?"

"You don't mean... Oh, no!" shrieked Ermintrude, "I forgot to organise the entire concert! It's a complete and utter DISASTER!"

Florence heard the commotion and came over to see what was wrong. "Whatever's the matter, Ermintrude?" she asked.

DIVA
CONCERT

"I put up the posters for my show but there's no show for anyone to see," sulked Ermintrude "I was so busy practising, I've forgotten to organise everything else."

"I'm sure Florence will know what to do!" said Brian helpfully.

Florence thought hard for a moment.

"What if Dylan played the guitar for you? And Dougal, the children and I can be your fans?" she wondered.

"Er, I'm a very busy dog today," said Dougal.

"Too busy for a sugar lump?" said Florence.

Dougal sighed. "Well, maybe I've just got time..."

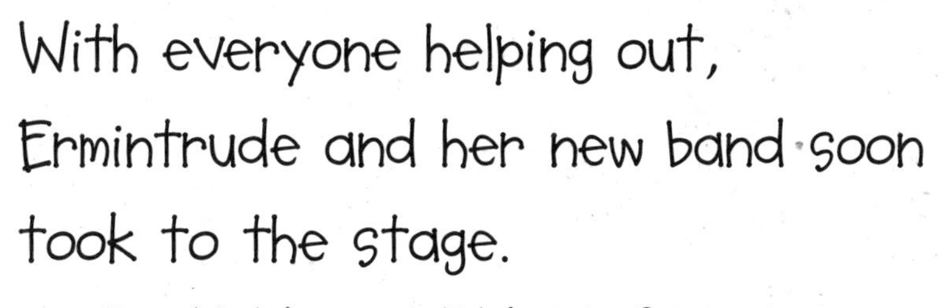

With everyone helping out, Ermintrude and her new band soon took to the stage.

"READY, EVERYONE?" she warbled. "One, two, three!"

Just as Ermintrude began to sing, Dylan's eyes fluttered and he fell fast asleep.

Ermintrude soon spotted Dylan dozing. Her eyes narrowed. She danced closer and closer and closer.

Dylan didn't move.

Ermintrude raised her tail and...

THWACK!

She swatted Dylan briskly on the back of the head!

"Whoa! Man!" he woke with a start. He grabbed his guitar and began to play an exceedingly loud tune.

"Dylan!" stormed Ermintrude.
"I am the star of this concert!"
She bawled, "EEEOOOOOOOOOO!"
even louder than before.

But Dylan was lost in his own music and the louder Ermintrude sang, the louder he played.

Dylan and Ermintrude got louder and louder and LOUDER!

Soon, the noise was **deafening!** The children looked at each other in shock. The lights wobbled and the stage shook.

Dougal ran away and hid.
"Stop!" shouted Florence.
"PLEASE STOP!"

Just as everyone thought their ears would explode...

BOING!

Zebedee arrived!

"What's all this racket?" he asked.

Suddenly, everything went quiet and everyone breathed a sigh of relief.

"Erm – we got a bit carried away there, didn't we?" said Ermintrude. "So sorry darlings!"

"Yeah, like, sorry dudes," said Dylan.

Looking very sorry indeed, Ermintrude said, "I shall dedicate my next song to Zebedee, Florence and all my lovely fans." She began singing a sweet lullaby in her most gentle voice.

When she had finished singing, Brian gave Ermintrude a pretty purple flower.

"Ooh, Ermintrude!" he blushed adoringly. "You're a STAR!"

THE MAGIC ROUNDABOUT™

Light Activated Room Guard DYLAN™

Gift Boxed Mugs

Bouncing ZEBEDEE™

Zebedee still has some spring in his step!

Character Beanies

Talking FLORENCE™

ERMINTRUDE™ Back Pack

Talk'n Sing ERMINTRUDE™

Remote Control DOUGAL™

Colour and specification may change.